Places to Be

Written by Mac Barnett

Illustrated by Renata Liwska

BALZER + BRAY
An Imprint of HarperCollinsPublishers

To Alessandra
—*M.B.*

To Michael, my travel companion
for all the places to be
—*R.L.*

Balzer + Bray is an imprint of HarperCollins Publishers.

Places to Be
Text copyright © 2017 by Mac Barnett
Illustrations copyright © 2017 by Renata Liwska

For information address HarperCollins Children's Books, a division of HarperCollins Publishers,
195 Broadway, New York, NY 10007.
www.harpercollinschildrens.com

ISBN 978-0-06-228621-5

The pictures in this book were made with brush and ink and digital hocus-pocus.
Typography by Dana Fritts
17 18 19 20 21 PC 10 9 8 7 6 5 4 3 2 1
❖
First Edition

Hurry up! We have places to be.

Places to be happy

and blue

and purple.

We have places to be tall

and places to be little.

Places to be loud

and awestruck

and cozy and warm.

We have places to be beastly.

We have places to be mad

and sweet

and thirsty.

You and I, we have so many places to be!

We have places to be brave.

We have places to be muddy

and funny

and lazy

and lovely.

We have places to be careful.

We have places to be bored.

We have places to be picky.

We have places to be sneaky

and places to be sleepy.

We have places to be acrobatic.

Places to be sullen

and scared

and scary.

We have places to be odd

and musical.

We have places to be jubilant.

Yes, we have so many places to be.

And I'll be with you,

and you'll be with me.